SHIVERS IN TIME

PJ SHERMAN

ISBN 978-0-244-73640-8

Table of Contents

Page Numbers:

Welcome

Oh, hello there. Pleasure to meet you. Please don't mind the mess, I've been a bit busy lately putting my life experiences down on paper.

Yes, that's right. They are for you, so I hope you enjoy. Remember, these are stories that should shake you to the core and challenge your perceptions and opinions.

There will be blood...

There will be ghosts and demons...

But I think...NO, I KNOW...that the scariest things that lie within this book of horror are human in nature.

What's scarier than knowing that any of this could happen to you?

Don't believe me? I shall think of you when you walk into the void, blissfully unaware of the dangers that await you...

The End of the Road

"Joanne, you get that story, or you're finished here. No more excuses."

The line goes dead. My boss can be a right asshole at times. I stare at the blank screen as worry starts to creep in, but I shake it off, adjust my hair in the rear-view mirror and open the car door.

The murder house is right in front of me; its plain, unassuming exterior shields the picturesque cul-de-sac from a bloodbath.

Or so I'm told...

I've got someone on the inside at the local Police Station. We go way back. I helped her out once at school and she's the type who always wants to repay a favour. A real Good Samaritan, which suits me fine, especially when I need access to the next breaking story. I'm in need of one after that phone call. Ever since school, I had always wanted a life in Journalism. How things change.

A chill goes through me as I take in the dystopian eyesore in front of me; the gnarled tree in the front garden that comes straight out of Sleepy Hollow; The lawn that looks like it hasn't been mown in a decade. The house stands out like a sore thumb against a neighbourhood teeming with white picket fences and manicured lawns.

My phone buzzes, bringing me back to reality. It's a text from Cody, my inside spy.

Sorry hon, I'm not at the scene. Let me know how it goes.

There are limitations to her usefulness after all. I roll my eyes and notice that I'm the only reporter here, the first one on scene. Silver linings and all that. I spot an Officer wandering about in the garden of the murder house, putting up yellow tape. I'm careful not to get my heels wet as I step over a puddle and cross the road towards him.

"Least the weather is holding up nicely for you Officer," I try to charm him, putting my teeth whitening sessions to good use. It's no use as he barely looks up at me, managing a quick glance, only really noticing the camera around my neck.

"You're a reporter?" I nod, my smile faltering. "No comment." He states matter of factly, turning his back on me. I bite my tongue - the temptation to introduce him to my wrath is difficult to suppress. I try a different, more direct tactic.

"Any info on the stiff then?" I ask casually, knowing it would prompt a reaction. I'm not wrong. He stops and stares at me for a few seconds, his face souring.

"The VICTIM is none of your concern." He turns his back on me, continuing with the tape. I take my chance and start snapping pictures of the murder house.

"Get any good pictures Miss?" A gruff voice behind me makes me jump. I laugh, clutching my hand to my chest in shock. A seventy something man with speckled hair and a handle bar moustache smiles at me. I marvel at how pristine his teeth are - we are equals on that front. His eyes twinkle magically. I notice he's slightly taller than me and his arms are quite thick for someone his age. He would have been quite the catch forty years ago. I return the smile, lowering my camera.

"Getting there. I need to speak to some locals and get an idea about the victim and what happened."

"I can help you there. I knew her very well."

"Her? I thought the Police hadn't revealed any details?"

"Word travels fast around here. Plus, I was in the area when it happened. You could call me a key witness." He winks before pointing at a little, green patch of land about two hundred yards down the road,

"I have an allotment. There's not much I don't see whilst spending time with Mother Nature." He takes out a handkerchief and blows into it, staring at me.

I notice the Officer looking at us. He seems entranced by the man, glancing down at his notepad and back at us, but doesn't write anything. "Do you know him?" I ask the old man. He shakes his head, "No. Anyway, walk with me. I've got things to finish on the allotment." He starts to amble off at a swift pace. I follow.

My phone buzzes again. It's Dad. I stop.

Mum's been rushed to hospital. I'll call if it's something serious.

"Everything okay?" The old man stares at me, whilst looking at the Officer every now and then. He seems in a rush.

"My Mum has cancer..." There's an awkward silence as the Old Man rubs his hands together. I shake my head, "I'm sorry, I don't know why I told you that. It's none of your concern." He nods, deep in thought.

"You should go to her. My wife had cancer. She's gone now." His face is emotionless as he stares blankly into space. I reach out and grab his hand and hold it tightly, smiling at him warmly, "I'm sorry to hear that. I'll go and see Mum after." We share a moment, blissfully staring into space, lost in our thoughts.

"Anyway!" I exclaim, snapping us both out of our day dreams, "Let's get this interview done. Actually, you didn't tell me your name?"

"No, I didn't." He casually ignores the question and continues walking towards the allotment. I crinkle my nose in amusement and continue following him. I appreciate the man's candour.

"Excuse me?" I hear a stern voice and look back. It's the Officer. He waves at me to come over. I mirror his rude waving with my own gesture, dismissing his beckoning.

"Miss, you shouldn't…" His voice fades away as I increase my pace to catch up with the Old Man, who steams ahead of me, defying his advancing years.

As we approach the allotment, I feel the faintest of rain drops hit my face. "Oh bugger!" I exclaim. The Old Man looks up, nonchalantly and shrugs. "It's only light." I nod, forcing a smile. I remove my notepad and unscrew my pen. I always carry the black, fountain. Anything else just screams amateur. As we're about to start, I almost forget the tape recorder. "Can I record this?" He nods his approval.

"So, let's start with the basics, what's your name?"

"We'll get to that. Next question." I get the sense he's telling me off. I pull my coat tighter. The wind is picking up.

"Okay, so how do you know the deceased? What's your relationship?"

"We live on the same street. Mrs Williams was an absolute busy body - nobody liked her." I look at him. The kind features look a little harsher now and his eyes, they don't twinkle so much. I push that to the back of my mind, I need to remain professional. This could be my big scoop. The rain starts to come down more heavily. I notice the Police Officer from earlier walking up towards us. The Old Man taps my arm and points to a shed,

"Come on, let's get out of the rain."

The Old Man slams the shed door behind me and walks over to a table in the corner. There's an old gas lamp and camp stove, which he turns on. "Tea?" I nod. He gestures to an old chair in the corner, "Please sit." I brush off the cobwebs and take a seat, adjusting myself a few times to make the hard wood a little more bearable. I place the recorder on the window sill that overlooks the allotment. The rain trickles down the glass. There's this musty smell I can't quite make out. I look at the Old Man as he busies himself with the stove.

"Does that Police Officer know you?" The Old Man shakes his head, "No. Must want a statement." His attention is divided between rifling through a drawer and staring out of the window.

"Are you looking for something or expecting someone?" He ignores me and continues the strange behaviour. He pulls something out of the drawer, but I can't see what it is. He walks over to the door and bolts it. I jump out of my seat.

"What are you doing!?" He turns around to face me. He's holding an old hand gun, the barrel staring me down. He cocks it and gestures to the seat. "Sit down please. I must confess. Tell the truth. You can help me with that." I sit and reach for the recorder.

"Leave it on," he commands.

"I didn't mean to kill her. It just happened. She wouldn't stop nagging. Thirty years of nagging..." The Old Man stands deathly still, staring through me as if talking to someone else. "You understand right? You know who I am now?"

I hadn't the foggiest, so return his stare blankly. He looks really angry now. "You kids with your degrees. Still dumb. My name is Geraint...Geraint Williams." My mouth drops in amazement. This cannot be happening, and I've got myself locked in a room with him.

"She was my wife, but she was also a right bitch. No one liked her. I was forced to marry her. I got her pregnant at fifteen and that was it in those days. My life was over. I've had to live with her and her constant moaning ever since. Then I find out she's been seeing the gardener. Forty-two years of age. How could I compete!? I just snapped." He rambles on, but that last sentence really annoys me.

"So, she didn't have cancer?" It was more of a rhetorical question as I stare at him, not believing the lies this man is capable of. "Why would you lie about that, you sick..."

He points the gun at me, "Shut your mouth. I am sick, you're right. I don't know what's going on up here anymore," he signals to his head, "They're running around up there, eating away..." I hold out my hands, nodding my head. I must try and make him believe I understand how he's feeling. All I want to do is get away from this psycho. I slowly get out of my seat and walk towards him.

"It's going to be okay. I can help you."

"Sit down!" He screams, taking a step forward. I shield my face and obey his command. If I'm to get out of this alive, I need to stay calm. There's a bang at the door and a familiar voice bellows,

"Open up Mr Williams. Leave the lady alone." Relief fills my every pore. After meeting the Officer, I never thought I'd end up glad to see him again. His voice causes the Old Man to start trembling. He turns to face me, takes three steps forward and reaches out to grab my hand. I scream, causing the Officer to continue hammering on the door.

The Old Man looks me in the eye and lifts the gun to his temple, "I'm sorry. I never meant for any of this to happen."

I try to stop him, but he curls his finger and it's all over.

A bang and his body slumps to the ground. I sit there for what feels like eternity as the hammering is drowned out by the overbearing sound of silence and my own thoughts.

I stir slightly as the door crashes open and the Officer rushes in. He checks I'm okay before inspecting the Old Man's body. My phone buzzes. It's a call. I take it out of my pocket and stare at the screen blankly.

It's Dad.

My day is about to get even worse.

The Winter Stranger

The snow crunched underfoot as I made my way back. It was the last of it, thankfully. I carved another line into Old Fir, the seventy something foot conifer that dominated the island's skyline. Even she was benefiting from the oncoming Spring, her once blanketed needles free again to point and prick any unsuspecting fauna that journeyed too close.

There were one thousand, one hundred and fifty-eight lines - including today's - that I had carved into Old Fir since The Event. It had changed everything for everyone, including my family. They didn't survive the first winter.

There was a rush of air and a flurry of black feathers as I felt Aves land on my shoulder, her talons making her presence known. She cawed in my ear and fixed her ebony eyes on the pouch that hung about my neck. She devoured the seeds instantly as I poured them into my open hand. Aves was my only friend in this bleak wilderness. After she had finished, she took off up to her nest in the loftiest branch of Old Fir.

I pushed open the cabin door, the smell of pine welcoming me home. After resting my bow by the table, I walked over to the radio in the corner and switched it on. Just like every other day, there was static. It was comforting to me, in a macabre way, that the Earth had peace at last. She could begin to heal. I emptied my pouch onto the table; meagre pickings. There was barely enough to last me the week, but that wasn't uncommon during winter. I had already started to see signs of some pack rats emerging from the old mine about two miles from here, keen to explore the returning warmth. I bit my bottom lip at the thought of a hot, cooked meal.

The snow crunched outside.

I froze, before reaching for my bow.

There was a flash by the window. I threw open the door, my bow ready to fire. But there was nothing. As I relaxed, I noticed some tracks in the snow - footprints. That was impossible, but I could see them leading up into the forest.

There was a crackle over the radio.

"There?"

My body went cold as the hair on my arms stood on end. This was not happening. I grabbed my pouch, kept my bow taught and left the cabin. I would follow the tracks. At my whistle, Aves came down from her nest and took point. She was more alert to danger than I ever could be.

We passed Old Fir and the fallen stump I frequently rested on, but nothing was out of the ordinary, except the tracks. They were clearly human, but they seemed smaller than mine. I could be seeing my own; the lack of fresh snow fall, coupled with my irrepressible hunger, could have caused me to hallucinate, imagining the flash at the window. But that voice on the radio - that voice was unmistakeable. I sat on the stump and closed my eyes. I had to regain my senses, as it was not the time to descend into madness.

Aves returned to me and dropped several red berries in my palm. I ate them with haste, closing my eyes as I savoured the taste. Despite them being bitter, the cranberries released a desperately needed energy resource. Aves pecked me lightly on the cheek and flapped her wings. She had found something. I picked up my bow and followed her.

After a good thirty minutes had passed, we arrived at a boggy patch of land, about the size of a football pitch. I dropped my head, resting it in my hands. I was so overjoyed, I was brought to tears. In front of us was a sea of red; at least ten thousand cranberries were ripe for picking, ready to save Aves and I from what had been an inevitable demise. I got to work, stuffing as many as I could into my pouch, as Aves circled above, maintaining a vigilant watch for bears.

As I slammed the cabin door shut, I eagerly made my way over to the chair by the fire to inspect my haul, Aves sat on my shoulder in anticipation of a feast. I opened the bulging pouch, conscious not to squash any of the precious cargo within. Both Aves and I indulged for a few moments, enjoying every bite and swallow. Fortunately, Aves' appetite wasn't as needy as mine, so she gave up half way through our binge and flew out of the window. It was getting dark.

The fire was roaring, my stomach was full, and Spring was on its way. I had survived another harsh winter, alone. This island had everything I could possibly need. I closed my eyes, smiling.

There was a crunch in the snow.

My eyes snapped open.

A knock at the door.

My heart sank, and my body went ice cold again.

As I slowly opened the cabin door and surveyed the darkness, I saw a small parcel. A note was attached. I unravelled the parcel - inside was a cooked pack rat. I unfolded the note;

You're not alone...

Fading Light

As I lay there, though my eyes are closed, I can see you. You recoil at the bite of my icy cold skin. It upsets me, but I understand - you're not used to seeing me like this. In this state.

A tear rolls down your flushed cheek, but you're too focussed on me to notice. I wish I could wipe it away for you. I see you're wearing the dress that I helped Dad pick out for you at that shop you love. It suits you. I do feel guilty for always teasing you about shopping there, but you never had the money to go elsewhere.

Something else I let you down on - the promise of giving you a comfortable life was swept away as my selfish needs came first. Again. Not that that ever changed your love for me - unwavering.

Graeme and Todd came by this morning - it's the first time I've seen either of them since the crash. They both came out okay - I don't resent them for that. They told me you felt differently though, that you weren't speaking to them - please don't blame them. I took the pills, it's my fault.

Even though I'm not here, the horrors of that night still haunt me - her eyes, Mum. Her eyes were the last thing I remember. What did I do? You won't mention it, but Graeme and Todd told me what I did.

That poor little girl.

Her family.

I'm a monster...

There's a figure in the shadows. I can see it in the corner of my eye. It's following me, watching me. I don't know what it wants Mum, but I don't like it. Is this my punishment? Please help me Mum.

Wait - it's telling me something. I think it wants me to go with it. I can't tell - its voice is distorted and hard to understand, like the sound of marbles rolling about in your hand.

I have to go now Mum. Take care of Dad.

The light is growing dimmer now. I'm following the figure - everything is fading, except the croaking. There's a horrible, musty smell, but I don't care. I don't even feel anymore. Why don't I feel?

It's dark now, so dark...

The Sins of the Mother

I had always thought myself different.

Strange in a way.

"Freak" they used to call me.

Some still do.

It was not until the day of my Mother's funeral did, I start to really appreciate what being different meant. As my boot crunched on the hard snow, I gazed across at the gaggle of disgusting human pigs that waddled towards my Mother's final resting place. To be accurate, she would be buried in a monumental palace of a family tomb, underneath the family estate. The hole in the ground and coffin that lay before us was merely part of the act. She always had an eye for theatrics and excess.

As the Vicar began his ramblings, I noticed that mine was the only dry eye. The fifty or so mourners that had turned up to feign sorrow were all wailing and fainting. Even the Vicar could smell gold and was ramping up the tears. I could sense their little, piggy eyes glancing over now and then, desperate for my attention. As I was the only heir to an enormous estate, young Master Rathbone was finally someone that everybody wanted to know. I had never wanted this life; privileged was what my Mother had always called me. She had detested me ever since my Father had left us when I was merely a child, as if my doughy eyes could have had any effect on his lust for my Nanny. She had quite coldly and with great joy informed me of his death a few years later. She was evil incarnate, and I couldn't have been happier to know she was now rotting and feeding the earth with her toxic being.

In the mix of the rabble, an older woman had caught my eye. She was unfamiliar to me and I had a memory for faces. Her hawkish eyes made coal look light and her tall, skeletal frame was hugged tightly by the most beautiful of black fabric.

I stand corrected – there was another dry eye.

"Your father is not dead. What your Mother told you was a load of nonsense." Gretchen Von Oosthuizen spat as she searched my face for weakness. I was not a very emotional person normally, however this revelation took me by surprise. I could feel my face tighten. The other guests noticed the minor change in my emotion as they shovelled their gluttonous 'after-party' spread down their cavernous holes, muttering between them.

They were so desperate.

"I'm…sorry?" I stuttered. She slapped my wrist quite forcefully. There was a gasp around the room and everyone stared. It was short-lived as Gretchen Von Oosthuizen fixed them with a withering look, causing the guests to return to their conversations. She returned her focus to me.

"Never apologise. Von Oosthuizen's are never wrong."

"Who are you?"

"Your grandma. Now stop with these foolish questions boy and take this." She thrust an envelope into my hands. The touch of the material was otherworldly. I felt both warmth and cold in tandem for a fleeting second before the questions became overwhelming and they flowed from my mouth.

"But my Father is dead? Why are you here now?"

Grandma Von Oosthuizen dismissed my questions with a swift move of her hand, her bony finger uncurling to stab at the envelope. Her stare bore into me, the dark eyes flashing a brilliant amethyst as the clitter-clatter of dinner plates softened into the background.

"Open the envelope. Your answers lay within." Her raspy voice echoed about my head.

"Seek us out when you are ready."

As I regained focus, Grandma Von Oosthuizen had vanished. The family lawyer was on stage, waiting for my focus to return. In her hand, she held a single piece of paper and her face was a melancholy one. All eyes were on me, but I had no idea what for. The family lawyer sensed my confusion, cleared her throat and repeated with venom,

"You're broke. There is no estate. Debts up to here."

She stretched her bloated arm to its extent above her head, only stopping her exaggerated action due to her ankles buckling from the weight.

As soon as the shock had dissipated, the guests' greedy eyes went blank. Within moments, they swarmed from the room, faster than they had arrived, clearly despondent that they couldn't pick clean from what remained of the Rathbone carcass. As the realisation came, I felt a great sense of relief and was more than happy to sign the papers the family lawyer had thrust in front of me. Everything was being handed over to the creditors. The Rathbones were done. But I wasn't a Rathbone any longer - was I?

I tore open the envelope, no longer concerned with the craftsmanship that had been invested to perfect such an insignificant item and pored over the letter within. The ink glistened as if the pen had only recently been removed from the paper. The hoarse voice of my recently discovered Grandma von Oosthuizen reverberated around my head.

The instructions were clear; I was to head to a small, seaside town in Wales called Tenby. Supposedly that was where my Father was and where my questions would find answers. Attached to the reverse of the letter was a train ticket. For the first time in my life, I felt a sense of purpose and my Rathbone identity had fortunately died with my mother, therefore there was nothing to keep me here. I marched from the building with vigour as those butterflies in my stomach performed acrobatics.

I watched the rain snake down the thick window of the carriage as we thundered along the Welsh countryside. Despite hearing tales of luscious green fields and an infinite bounty of nature's greatest assets, Wales was turning out to be a very macabre and gloomy place. The family that sat opposite paid no favours to my prejudice as they glared at me, their grubby clothes making my nose turn. I forced a smile to lighten the mood but received nothing in return. I turned back towards the window and found some solace in the wicked weather, hoping that we would arrive in Tenby soon.

That feeling was perhaps premature as a very pretty girl opened the door of our carriage; no sooner had I inhaled sharply at her beauty that the entire family opposite was jostled out of the door by the Father, who shot a pitying look my way before slamming the door behind us.

The pretty girl smiled, walked over to the seat in front of me and sat down. As she stared out of the window, also tracing the droplets as they moved down the window, I couldn't help but notice how she looked; her blue & white striped dress came down to her knees, as did her straw-coloured hair, which bounced with every breath she took. Her eyes were a brilliant green, which made it impossible not to stare into them. After nervously glancing back at me a few times, she caught me staring and started to play with the hem of her dress. She looked up and fixed those stunning eyes onto me,

"Can I help you sir?" she had the most angelic voice, with the slightest twang of a Welsh accent. I had lost the ability to

speak and merely garbled and shook my head side to side.
She giggled innocently and kicked her legs,

"You've gone a funny shade of red, sir."

I took a deep breath to regain my nerve and swallowed.

"Yes, yes. I'm sorry. Not sure what came over me." I paused
and dabbed my brow as she continued to look at me. How
strange she must have thought I was.

"Are you visiting family, sir?"

"Yes, indeed I am. You?"

She nodded and bit her bottom lip. We stared at each other
for a few minutes before I felt the train come to a stop. With
that, she jumped from her seat, wished me a quick goodbye
and exited the carriage. I shook my head in disbelief;
naturally I was upset that I didn't have the courage to ask her
name, but also happy that this journey was over.

As I stepped out of the carriage, I was forced to hug my thick
coat closer as an arctic wind swept across the platform,

causing the lantern of the Station Master's office to crash to the floor and extinguish the only source of light. I watched as an elderly lady was pushed into the arms of a portly gentleman that had been taking cover from the elements. I couldn't tell if the loud crack that followed was her breaking something or part of the wind's cruel game to frighten us further. I thought of the pretty girl in my carriage and how she was faring in this weather but could not make her out in this storm. She was not my problem – my problem – was to find my Father and to find a cab. It wasn't until the grizzly looking oaf that drove the cab demanded money upfront did I once again remember my predicament. I was penniless.

"I'm terribly sorry," I stammered. He could sense my embarrassment, but that only made him angrier. He bellowed at me in a thick, welsh accent,

"Stop wastin' my time. Clear orf and make room for payin' customers!" I couldn't tell if he was shouting because he was annoyed or, so he could be heard over the crashing of the wind and the waves. We were only feet away from the shore and the sea spray was relentless in its pursuit to drown us. I yelled as loudly as possible,

"I need to get to Waterford House."

What I could see of his face under the hood changed dramatically at those words. Even his horse started to pant and dance on the spot. He would no longer look me in the eye and only pointed to an imposing house on top of a hill in the distance. No sooner had the gratitude left my lips did he whip his horse and the carriage flew out of sight leaving flecks of dirt across my face.

Fortunately, I had packed light, so the harsh incline to the top of the hill wasn't too arduous. As I was never one for physical exertion, it brought a sweat to my brow, which didn't last long as the storm washed it from my face. I would only be a sopping wet new addition to the von Oosthuizen family, rather than a muddy and grubby one too.

Waterford House was an imposing colossus of brick and stone; from what I could make out from the brief visibility that the lightning overhead provided, there were three towers that ran the length of the house, jagged and pointed at the top, each one larger than the last. I was surprised if upon closer inspection there wasn't a sleeping beauty ready to be rescued. I ran my fore finger across one of the two, brass knockers that were attached to the two imposing, wooden doors that towered at least another three feet above me. I recoiled at the touch – the otherworldly and icy sensation reminded me of the letter. I swallowed and composed myself and after providing some much-needed self-motivation, my new-found courage enabled me to grasp hold of the knocker and swing.

Once.

Twice.

Thr-...

Before I had finished the third swing, the doors began to creak open.

What met my eyes was strange, yet not wholly unexpected based on my previous encounter with Grandma von Oosthuizen; a sliver of candle light illuminated my feet, but as I rose my head to peer into the murky darkness, I saw the outline of two hulking beasts snorting down at me, their breath heavy and coming in short, angry bursts. I took a step back, slipped and the last thing I remember was hitting my head. The dark grew darker.

As I stirred, my eyes remained shut, but I could hear the faint whisper of voices around me.

"He must be ready…"

"There cannot be a single drop wasted…"

"Quickly! Father is waiting to rise."

My eyes slowly began to open, letting the faintest of light in. Standing at the foot of my bed were the two large creatures that had greeted me at the front door; their gorilla frames and buck teeth were a strange contrast to the beautiful and mesmerising blonde hair that cascaded down their thick torsos. These women were identical in every way, except the chains that hung about their fat necks. At the end of one was a golden goat and the other a golden dagger. I lifted my head to look around but couldn't make much out in the darkness; a solitary candle provided some light.

"Who are you?"

The twins unfolded their arms in unison and pointed to a chair in the corner, which had a neatly folded pile of clothes. It was only then that I realised I was naked.

"Where are my clothes?"

"Change now." The one on the left grunted. The one on the right snorted her approval. They sensed my hesitation, and both took a step forward roaring at me,

"CHANGE! NOW!"

I leapt from the bed towards the chair, desperately attempting to protect what dignity remained and started to unfold the clothes; there was a long, silk robe that seemed to emit a strong purple glow, despite the low lighting, a pair of equally silky and purple elbow length gloves and a blindfold. Not wanting to antagonise the hulking beasts in the corner any further, I pulled the robe over my head, slipped on the gloves and placed the blindfold over my face. I felt an enormous, hairy hand grab my shoulder, almost crushing it as I was bundled
out of the room.

The blindfold omitted my vision, but I could feel the icy cold bite of the marble beneath my bare feet. I heard the creak of doors opening towards my mysterious destination, shuffling feet and heavy breathing, which was overpowered by a familiar smell of burning wood and another scent I couldn't quite place. My memory teleported me temporarily to when I had gashed my leg upon a rock as I climbed around the cliffs in my teens and the family doctor had to cauterise it to stem the flow. I scoffed at the possibility of it being the smell of seared flesh.

When I finally came to a stop, it was upon what felt like cold, wet stone. A familiar hoarse voice barked somewhere in front of me and the voice echoed, like in a cave.

"Remove his blindfold."

As it was lifted from my face, my eyes didn't need much adjustment; I was stood in a cave with the light as low as the rest of the house and a howling wind battered through the cave, causing the tiny droplets that fell from the stalactites to echo loudly. In the distance the sea and its waves crashing into the cave's entrance were visible, but we seemed to be protected from the freezing chill that had greeted me earlier this evening, as if in some magical bubble. In the centre of the cave was a circle of strange symbols that had been etched into the ground and stood just above it on a makeshift pedestal was Grandma von Oosthuizen, dressed in a robe like mine.

"What is going on?" I yelled at her, taking a step forward. I felt the twins' heavy hands about my shoulders, but Grandma von Oosthuizen shook her head. I was released and took another step forward. She eyed me with great interest, licking her lips in the process. A shiver ran up my spine and the hair on my arms stood to attention.

"We are welcoming..." she started with a cool and confident manner, the words slowly making their way off her thin lips.

"...a new member to the family."

I took another step forward, inches from the centre circle. Her eyes narrowed, and the twins dragged me back swiftly. I shook them off with a newly found sense of purpose.

"This is hardly the normal way to introduce someone to the family. I've only just met you and you're already parading me around nearly naked in some oddball fancy dress. Is this some joke? I don't want to join the family if this is how you're going to behave..."

Grandma von Oosthuizen's bird like gaze never faltered. She threw back her head and cackled loudly.

"Oh, my dear boy, you honestly believe that's you? You were an easy recruit..." She gestured to the twins, "Bring out the girl."

With my mouth agape, I stared in disbelief as the young girl from the train, was brought into the cave. She too was wearing a similar robe, but hers was pure white. There was no fear or trepidation. There was even a hint of a smile as she side glanced at me and winked. She leaned in and softly whispered in my ear,

"Well this is awkward." She walked into the centre circle and was disrobed, her silky skin glimmered in the candle light.

"Bring the sacrifice," Grandma von Oosthuizen commanded. I felt my feet leave the floor before being forced by the twins onto my knees in front of the young girl. I turned my head with as much force as possible, so I could see the old witch that stood above us and to protect the girl's dignity.

"Where's my Father?"

Grandma von Oosthuizen's face cracked as a sinister smile grew across her face, a shark would have been jealous of the pointy teeth that lined her gums.

"Your Father is dead."

She relished in the confusion on my face. "You are the last of your family. We needed your blood to complete the ritual.

That's why I visited you. You were so gullible, so desperate to find your Father."

She leaned forward on her platform, those eyes as black as any mining pit.

"Your Mother was responsible for this. She had your Father come to us, but his blood wasn't strong enough. You were the next best she could offer to continue her life of riches."

I was too shocked to ask any further. My lip quivered, and my eyes rolled in their sockets, desperately searching for an answer to this most hideous of natural treachery.

"Faust, my dear boy. Faust."

Grandma von Oosthuizen removed a steel dagger from beneath her cloak as she made her way down to the centre circle; something slithered across its matte black surface in the dull light as she held it above the girl's head. I tried to scream, to protect the girl, but was paralysed. The girl raised her hands and smiled, welcoming her fate as the knife came down and slashed across them. My face splattered with crimson. The girl turned to me, her face had lost its innocence and was now maniacal, feral. Her hands had been cut deep from the blade, but it was as if she felt nothing.

I tried to struggle again against the twins, but I could barely manage to turn my head as I saw Grandma von Oosthuizen gift the girl the dagger, who brought it above my head with an upswing dripping in ecstasy.

The girl stopped, the dagger inches above my forehead. Her face softened slightly at the sight of my tears. She bent down. I could feel her cold breath on my face. Her tongue reached out and licked the tears from my cheeks. The girl closed her eyes to savour the taste.

With that, the last thing I remember was a searing, splitting pain in my forehead and the sight of two scaly feet emerge from the centre circle. A deep, rumbling voice spoke a language I'd never heard before as my blood slowly pooled around my face...

Click

Buzz.

I ignored it.

Buzz.

I rolled my eyes and flipped the phone over. I could resist its bee impression, but the flashing light was too much.

Buzz.

Buzz.

Buzz.

I slammed my pen down. Tea sloshed around the mug. Eyes widening, I willed the dark liquid to remain in its ceramic prison. Another mess to clean up was not what I needed now.

The incessant buzzing broke its routine as I flipped the phone onto its back. It was rewarding me for not going too long without a social media fix. There were five messages. FIVE.

It was Pete. Why Pete? My thumb hovered over the unlock button. Had it got hotter in here?

Click.

Unlocked.

Sweat snaked down my forehead, pooling above my eyebrow. The mug was at my mouth, lips slurping as I took a gulp. Tea tasted terrible cold.

Buzz.

I stared at the notifications. They weren't going away.

The slider moved across the screen with the slightest of resistance, the behaviour of a puppy when brought to the vet.

Click.

Opened.

A wink face.

Click. Click. Click.

Back went my reply.

Hey Pete – you okay?

Buzz.

Thumbs up. Another wink face.

Click. Click. Click.

Why do you keep winking?

The screen dimmed as I waited. And waited. The three dots
to say he was writing flashed up, then disappeared. Then
flashed. Then disappeared.

Click. Click. Click.

I sent a solitary question mark. I stared at my phone. Again, the screen grew dim. By the end of the night I would have no fingernails left.

The three dots again.

I fanned my face with a textbook. I had to take a layer off. The jumper hit the opposite wall with a thud. I didn't want to miss the reply.

"Honey, are you okay? I heard a noise." Mum's sickly-sweet voice wafted through the door. My nose crinkled.

"Yes Mum. Fine!"

"Okay, tea won't be long."

I gave my Mum the two fingered salute. She was always interrupting. Never any peace in this house.

Buzz.

Didn't put you down as a PE girl...

Buzz.

Another wink face.

I couldn't take another layer off. I rushed over and yanked open the window and sat on the sill, furiously typing.

Click. Click. Click.

What do you mean? Pete, you're being a weirdo. Like, stop it now.

The three dots. Oscillating across the screen, enjoying the torture they dished out. You never knew when they were going to strike. When the three dots stopped bouncing, you would either feel great joy, sadness or fear. Like a cruel game of spin the bottle.

Buzz.

Sad face.

Is that why you never dated me? You prefer older men?

Fortunately, pillows were there to soften the blow as the phone catapulted across the room.

Buzz.

Buzz.

Buzz.

I started to pace. Pacing jogged the mind, made the juices flow. The breathing techniques helped.

Breathe in...

My eyes wouldn't stop looking over. I was an addict.

Breathe in...

Breathe out...

It was no use. I had to face this. What did Pete know? A step on the stairs creaked. My pacing stopped.

"O-K Mum. Stop spying on me!"

Silence. I paused, finally able to breathe normally.

"Sorry honey. You don't want your tea to go cold." The stair creaked again. I resumed my pacing. I went back to my desk and opened the laptop, switching between various social media accounts. There were no posts, no videos, no pictures. Pete's profiles were littered with cat memes. And he wondered why I always said no.

Buzz.

The inner cobra in me danced about the bed, as I waited for the opportune moment to strike.

Now.

I grabbed the phone and unlocked. 4 messages. Mainly emojis. I shouldn't have picked it up. There was a picture message. Mr Fairchild and I looked so cute together. It was a shame really. Was Pete stalking me? My fingers set the screen on fire.

Click. Click. Click.

How did you know?

The three dots.

Thought you'd gone cold on me.

Click. Click. Click.

Were you stalking me?

The three dots.

Always. Wink face.

The three dots.

Do you like the scenes in all those horror movies where the hot chick is in her bedroom and the killer is in the wardrobe?

My eyes were on the wardrobe, searching for any movement. Without losing focus, my fingers tapped again.

Click. Click. Click.

Not funny.

The three dots.

Neither is this.

A picture message.

My hand went straight to my mouth to stop the scream. I felt like I was going to throw up. No one except Mr Fairchild and I knew about my secret getaway. He always thought it cute that I'd painted it sunshine yellow. The surrounding ferns provided ample protection for our midnight frolics.

The three dots.

I know what you did. I want something from you.

The three dots.

Smiley devil face.

The three dots.

Come alone. Now. I'll be waiting.

There was no time for a jacket as the back door slammed behind me, my Mother's complaints a distant memory as I hammered my bike's pedals with every bit of force I could muster. What I needed was there. It was still there from before.

Click. Click. Click.

Where are you?

The autumnal breeze blew the honey-coloured leaves across the front of the sunflower cabin, the stench of lavender causing me to wretch again as my head turned left and right, waiting for a sign of Pete. The lavender was a great touch though. Very strong odour.

The three dots.

Boo.

A hand caressed my shoulder, sending shivers down my spine. I dropped my bike and spun around. Pete's face was closer to mine than Kanye was to Kim. Even the lavender couldn't disguise what came from the pit of death called a mouth of his. I recoiled. He grabbed me by the elbow.

"I saw you and Mr Fairchild."

"And? What of it?" I struggled. He wore that tatty Rugby jacket, hiding the bulk underneath. His grip was solid, my bones felt like they were dismantling.

"You're hurting me…"

The darkness in his eyes started to fade as the pupils grew larger. He looked down. A flush of pink in his chubby cheeks.

Time for the cobra to strike.

"I'm sorry. I just really like you."

"What exactly did you see Pete?" He didn't look up, thrusting his phone into my hand.

Someone turned on my emotion tap as the fear drained, my estranged confidence returning. There were only pictures of a brief embrace between me and Mr Fairchild. Nothing here that would reveal the insidious truth. I looked back at Pete.

"Go home."

His emerald eyes brimmed with tears. A giant baby really. Too simple to understand life. My natural instincts were screaming at me as I placed my hand on his shoulder. A little bit of comfort would work. It did. He smiled and nodded.

As he turned to walk away, I breathed a sigh of relief and moved back to my bike. There was dirt all up the handle.

Click.

I froze.

That was the cabin door.

I gave him the opportunity. It was the only choice I had.

"Go in Pete."

"What's in there? It smells…" His arm shielded his nose as he poked the door open further.

"Go in Pete." I repeated, more forcefully.

He took a step forward. What I needed was inside. He took a second step – he was inside. I stalked behind him, my slight frame making no noise on the crunchy leaves beneath our feet. The bag was just inside the door. It was in arm's reach.

I stretched.

He took a few more steps forward.

"Oh. The smell. It's like…"

"Rotting flesh?" I giggled.

He stopped dead. Too late. He had seen Mr Fairchilds.
Lifeless. Blank stare. Cracked skull.

"What…happened…?"

"I told him to leave her. I loved him. She didn't. I deserved
him. She didn't. Too late for him now. And you…"

I felt the cold metal in my hand and gripped hard. It came
down once, twice, thrice…I lost count.

There was just a lot of Pete around the cabin. Turns out he
had a brain after all.

The oil sloshed about in the can as I shook it vigorously, ensuring both bodies were covered in the stuff. There could be no evidence. I had been invited to Cambridge after all. The feel of the lighter was so empowering. Its flame was entrancing as it danced on the spot, goading me to finish the act. I did. The cabin started to roar, and the heat was unbearable. I moved back to my bike.

There was a murmur. A muffled voice. Familiar. I searched the clearing. There was a light in the distance.

My phone.

I reached down. A picture of Mum grinning greeted me. She had been on the phone for at least ten minutes.

"Mum?"

"You need to get home. Now."

I turned to face the inferno and smiled. I would deal with Mother next. What a fun night this was turning out to be.

The Cemetery Bookshop

The dense fog lingered over Raspbone Manor, smothering the house; it permitted no sliver of the moonlight through its suffocating wall, laying a cover of pitch black across the grounds for at least a mile around. The pitter-patter of tiny rodents' feet echoed across the stone courtyard but could only be heard intermittently as the whispering wind pushed and prodded the solitary, open window of a bedroom on the upper-east side, causing it to clatter in the night.

A light went on as footsteps shuffled down the hallway towards the noise. Dressed in a flowing silk dressing gown, Lord Raspbone stopped outside the bedroom door; he looked up and down the corridor as if expecting someone. His bushy eyebrows quivered. Silence. He reached for the handle and turned it slightly. The wind had eased, but the window still crashed against the wall. Lord Raspbone reached for the light switch and flicked it.

Once.

Twice.

Nothing.

He hobbled across the wooden floor, towards the open window. A tiny light flashed into the room, causing his pupils to contract. He licked his lips and coughed, lifting his liver spotted hand to wipe the spittle from his wrinkled chin. Lord Raspbone held the window open with one hand and peered into the dark towards the light, the wind causing the hairs on his arms to raise. His dark eyes flashed, his skin turning a deathly white as he took a step back. There she was again. Staring at him. The face that never let him forget.

"No. Not again..."

He turned and marched, with great difficulty, over to a dressing table in the corner of the spacious room, picked up the phone and began to prod in the numbers. Every time he entered a new digit, he would look back out of the window at the face across the courtyard.

"Blast that bookshop. You will leave me alone!" He pointed threateningly at the building, as the phone started to dial.

There was a click on the other side.

"Yes, is that Miss Davids? I've changed my mind. I want to sell, no, need to sell Cemetery Bookshop. You should come in the morning. Yes, Goodnight."

Lord Raspbone returned the phone and backed away from the window, leaving it open as the silhouette in the building across the courtyard faded into the darkness.

*   *   *

"Look, I'm going to have to miss tonight...Yes, I'm aware it's the third time...Rosie. Stop shouting. I have to get this place otherwise Graham is going to fire me. You've met him. You know what he's like. Okay – I'll try and come back tonight, but it's a four-hour drive. No promises. Yes, love you too. Look, I've got to go, Graham is on the other line. Bye."

Fleur's finger pushed the button on her headpiece. It beeped, and the line clicked. Her lips pursed as her knuckles tightened around the steering wheel. The voice that escaped her mouth did not match the expression on her face.

"Hi Graham. How are-...yes, I'm on my way there now. Should be about another hour. Yes, I'm aware bonus season is coming up, I have worked for you for fourteen years-No, I wasn't being funny. Yes, I'll let you know when I've spoken with the client...Graham?"

The line clicked again. Fleur took a deep breath and pulled the car into a layby, before letting her head hit the steering wheel repeatedly, while an agonising moan seeped from her like steam from a freshly boiled kettle. She remained there for a few minutes before a loud knock on the window jolted her. A Police Officer had his face pressed against the glass, his breath creating a smudge as he inhaled and exhaled with great force. The window went down as Fleur stared at him. Silence descended as neither one spoke. Fleur's expression changed rapidly, her forehead loosening whilst her eyebrow raised.

"Can I help you Officer?"

"Yes, Miss. Just wanted to make sure you were okay. Making quite a racket you were, banging your head like that. Could have done yourself some damage."

"How did you hear me? We're miles from anywhere." Fleur looked around, giving her time to finally take in her surroundings; the rolling fields of green and yellow brought a smile to her face as the fresh smell of honeysuckle flicked at her nostrils. The Officer smiled before leaning through the window. Fleur fidgeted in her seat, pushing herself away from the Officer, watching him suspiciously.

"Beautiful place isn't it? Lived here all my life."

"Yes, very. Could you just back up please Officer? You're a little close."

The Officer looked down and laughed, before taking his hands off the car.

"Oops. Any-hoo, what are you here for Miss? Sampling our famous Cider? Enjoying the cliff walks?"

Fleur shook her head as she reached into her handbag. The Officer continued to smile as she pulled out her phone. A dark look came across the Officer's face as Fleur showed him a picture.

"I'm heading to Raspbone Manor to see the Cemetery Bookshop."

"Why would you want to go there?" His disposition had grown icy, the beaming smile a distant memory. Fleur hesitated. The Officer's upper lip started to curl as he craned his neck towards the car,

"You're from that company, aren't you?"

"Which company?" Fleur's eyebrow raised, her tone growing shorter.

"Don't be coy with me Miss. You know which one I'm talking about. Which one we're both talking about. It's the last bit of locally owned history we have, and you want to take that from us, tear it down and turn it into some holiday park. Not on our watch. No sir."

He straightened up, brushing his uniform down, eyes darting back and forth. Fleur noticed that the sun was now engulfed in rolling, black clouds and a wind had picked up. She pulled her coat tighter and went to wind up the window. The Officer's hands slammed down, causing her to jump. He leaned in as close as possible, piercing green eyes staring at her, unblinking. He took a breath and spoke very clearly with a slight growl,

"I am the friendliest person you're going to meet whilst you're here Miss Davids. Just remember that." The stare lingered before he removed his hands. Fleur clicked the button, breathing heavily. She looked in the rear-view mirror and watched the Officer walk back to his car, before starting the engine and speeding away with such force it caused the wooden sign post adjacent to the layby, to shake violently. Fleur peered up at it in the darkness.

The Village – 10 miles.

She shivered, before getting the car started and pulled away as the thick fog descended onto the road.

*   *   *   *

The thick smoke snaked slowly across the bar, providing Fleur with some privacy from the onslaught of beady eyes that stared at her from all corners of the room. She waved it away and coughed, trying to make eye contact with the pub Landlord as he made idle conversation with one of his elderly patrons, who was one of several that puffed away on a pipe.

"Sure that's illegal," Fleur muttered, pushing around in her handbag before pulling out an inhaler and taking two blasts. She held up her hand towards the Landlord and beckoned him over. He angled his head slightly to the side, looked Fleur up and down. The Landlord and his elderly patron looked at each other and chuckled, sneers on their faces as they continued to stare at Fleur, muttering.

Fleur held her head back and took a deep breath and closed her eyes. It was times like these that she really needed Rosie's sunny disposition and felt a little guilty about missing so many of their wedding preparation events. She smiled slightly at her phone's wallpaper; her and Rosie were holding hands while on holiday in Orlando. Fleur couldn't stop staring at it.

"That your friend?"

Fleur jumped. The Police Officer from earlier loomed over her, staring at Fleur's phone. She pocketed it swiftly and looked away.

"Yes. Something like that."

He continued to stand there. Fleur could make out his clown like feet bobbing up and down in unison, the black brogues squeaking. She looked back over at the Landlord.

"Excuse me. I need a room."

The Landlord noticed the Police Officer and made his way over.

"Alrigh' Officer Thomas? Gettin' dark now innit?"

Officer Thomas nodded before shifting his eyes from Fleur to the Landlord, who shook his head, lips pursed.

"Any rooms Frank?"

The Landlord's eyes narrowed, and the pub went deathly silent.

"No…" He looked at Fleur, "Fully booked."

Fleur looked from Officer Thomas to Frank and then to the eyes of the customers that had not stopped staring at her since she had entered. She was met with vacant faces. Fleur kicked her stool back, threw her coat around her shoulders and swung her handbag so violently, Officer Thomas had to duck.

"Watch it Miss Davids."

"No, you watch it." She poked his chest, causing him to wince.

"I am here to buy the Cemetery Bookshop and finish this job. This whole town has been nothing but rude and inhospitable towards me and my company. We saved this town and you were all too grateful to take our money. Well this is the final piece of the puzzle and you will have that luxury holiday park bringing all those lovely, inquisitive tourists to your back doors." She looked around the room, her look dared anyone to answer back. When she was satisfied, she nodded and turned to leave.

Officer Thomas grabbed her arm as she marched towards the door. Fleur looked down at his hand, before turning her glare towards the Officer.

"Let. Me. Go."

"There's a storm coming Miss Davids and there's only one rickety, old bridge up to Raspbone Manor. It's too dangerous."

Fleur took a breath and bit her lip, her eyes sweeping the room. She yanked her arm from the Officer's grasp.

"It's safer out there than it is here."

Fleur looked around the room, taking care to stare down every single customer one last time, before turning on the spot and exiting the pub, leaving the murmur of chatter to restart as if nothing had happened.

*   *   *   *

The windscreen wipers could barely deal with the force of the rain as it battered the car, causing Fleur to huddle very closely to the steering wheel, peering through the elements that blanketed the road in front of her. Out of nowhere, a bridge came into view; dominating the skyline, it provided the only route to Raspbone Manor across the river.

It creaked and moaned, exacerbated by the wind, as Fleur edged the car across. Her knuckles were white as she bit down hard on her bottom lip.

The bridge shuddered, throwing the car off route. Fleur had to swing the steering wheel hard to the right to prevent the car from crashing through the barrier and into the icy waters below. She then smashed her foot to the floor. The car jerked back into life and hared across the end of the bridge as the whole structure collapsed behind her. She stared into the rear-view mirror, eyes wide and pupils like pin pricks before stopping and reaching for her phone.

"Damn it." Her phone had no service. She tossed it back onto the passenger seat and continued to drive as a peeling sign swung in the wind, welcoming her to Raspbone Manor. Fleur could feel her hands shaking as she trundled through a tall, wrought iron gate and up the winding path, the Manor in the distance. About a hundred yards in front of her was another building, surrounded by a six-foot wall. She pulled over and wound down the window to light a cigarette. After a few drags, she started to cough and reached for her inhaler, taking a few puffs. She couldn't quite make out the name written across the building, but its large bay windows and distinctive red brick were familiar to her. After all, she had been staring at the blueprints for the past eighteen months.

She smiled, taking another drag on the cigarette. The coughing returned, and she glared at it, "You'll be the death of me…" Fleur stopped mid-sentence. The wind was still, as complete silence surrounded her. Then a low, croaking drifted across the air and a light scraping on the gravel caused her to look about. She could see no movement in the dark. Fleur noticed a flickering light from one of the bay windows and craned her neck forward.

Bang.

"Shit!"

Fleur dove into the back seat as there were a further two taps on the window.

"Hello? Are you okay?" A muffled voice shouted from outside. Fleur popped her head up and saw the outline of an elderly man. Laughing, her hand went to her chest in relief before she opened the rear passenger door and hopped out.

"I'm sorry, I didn't mean to startle you. You must be Miss Davids? Lord Raspbone at your service." The elderly gentleman held out his bony hand and Fleur grabbed it and shook strongly, afraid she might break his fragile frame.

"I thought I saw…Never mind."

"What?"

Fleur looked back at the Cemetery Bookshop, quiet and still. She shook her head.

"Nothing."

Lord Raspbone smiled, revealing a pristine set of teeth.

"Let's get you inside then and make you a nice cup of tea."
He signalled at the car, "Leave your bags. I'll have someone
fetch your things later."

With that, Fleur followed him to the Manor, taking one last
time to look back at the bookshop.

*   *   *   *

Fleur looked tentatively around the kitchen as Lord Raspbone
busied himself, fumbling around; oddly matched cupboard
doors with ornately decorated handles painted a picture of
mad exuberance; there was no sign of modern technology or
creature comforts as Fleur's host heaved a matte black, cast
iron kettle onto an old-fashioned cooker and spent several
minutes thumbing around drawers.

"I can never find those blasted matches. Where did she put
them?"

"She?"

Fleur paused and listened. The house was silent apart from the whisper of the wind that scratched at the tiny, four-paned kitchen windows.

"Hmm?" Lord Raspbone looked up, eyes unblinking and yellowish.

"You said she. Does someone else live here?"

He paused, and his eyes rolled side to side, as if searching for something. After a few moments, he shook his head and continued to make the tea.

"Oh no. Just me…"

There was a creak from one of the upstairs floorboards. Both looked up. Lord Raspbone pulled a strange grin, once again showing off those perfect teeth.

"...and the wind." He turned his back to Fleur and started to pour the hot water, continuing to chat away.

"It has been me for the last ten years, ever since..." He paused as his head dropped.

"The fire?" Fleur offered. Lord Raspbone continued to stand in silence. Fleur checked her phone. Still no signal. She jumped as a large, ceramic mug was slammed down in front of her. Lord Raspbone sat down opposite and peered over the top of his china cup and saucer, taking delicate sips. After several moments, Fleur pulled a tablet from her handbag and offered it to Lord Raspbone, who eyed it incredulously.

"Tell me Miss Davids, do I look like the typical millennial client you deal with?"

Fleur held the tablet in mid-air, mouth open.

"I'm sorry?"

Lord Raspbone placed the cup on the saucer and sighed.

"Paper, Miss Davids. Do you remember what that is? I like to feel the document that's about to decimate my livelihood and family history."

Fleur started to dig around in her handbag, Lord Raspbone looking on sullenly. She dropped the document file as she pulled it from her bag, placing her hand on her forehead.

"Everything okay Miss Davids?"

"Yes, yes. Just felt a little funny then."

"Have more tea." Lord Raspbone gestured at the mug, whilst eyeing the clock on the wall.

Fleur picked up her overtly large mug and took several more gulps as her host started to thumb through the documents, sighing at every turn.

"This won't do. You are vultures, picking the last remaining bits of flesh you can find. Vultures." Lord Raspbone hurled the document at Fleur's head, catching her on the cheek. Such was the force, it knocked her off the chair and sent her crashing to the ground. Head spinning, Fleur grabbed the chair and hoisted herself back onto her feet.

"What's wrong with you?" She slurred as her legs started to buckle beneath her. Her focus went to the contents of her mug, which now had a strange, black tint.

"My tea...you..."

Lord Raspbone drifted around the table towards her, concern written on his face. He grabbed Fleur by the elbow to support her as she dropped to her knees.

"I had no intention of selling to you. I needed you. My loved ones need to be freed. This isn't personal."

"You're...insane." Fleur could feel the room spinning as her head hit the cold, linoleum.

*   *   *   *

A draft howled under the thick, wooden door that had just been bolted from the outside; the scratching at the window as the overhanging trees brushed against the bookshop's walls, mixed with the tiny pitter-patter of scurrying feet in the darkness brought Fleur back to her senses. The musty stench of aged wood and burned candle wax caused her to wipe her eyes several times and cough violently. Fleur at up and started to panic, patting herself all over, before she pulled out her inhaler and took several, sharp blasts. A letter box that sat at the top of the door unbolted and opened with a clunk, a familiar pair of old, yellowish eyes peering in. Fleur found her balance and ran at the door, banging her fists hard on its surface.

"Let me out, now you jumped up jailor. I'll call the Police and bring the blue fury down on you, believe me."

Lord Raspbone sighed.

"And how exactly will you do that?" Fleur's hands went straight to her pockets and started to pat herself down again. The sudden realisation dawned on her as she took a few steps backwards. Fleur looked up at Lord Raspbone, confusion lining her face.

"Why?"

"My girls. She needs to feed." The desperation and fear were clear in his voice as it trembled. He paused.

"I'm sorry."

With that, he slammed the letter box, leaving Fleur in pitch black, except for a sliver of light from a lone candle that hanged above the door. The pitter-patter of scurrying feet stopped suddenly as the draft under the door grew stronger. Fleur jumped to her feet, still nursing the back of her head and reached for the candle, its wax dribbled down the side at every movement.

She turned to face the room, holding the candle out; in the darkness, she could see outlines of bookshelves that ran along the walls and down the middle. The ceiling was so high, she couldn't see it in this light. Draped across the empty walls were tattered, moth eaten banners that had once been brilliant emerald and gold but had now faded into obscurity.

Fleur reached out and touched one of the banners, dust spraying everywhere. She looked away to shield her face; the candle light illuminated a collection of old picture frames that hanged on the wall opposite. As she got closer, the outline of a plaque came into focus. Fleur reached out and wiped away the layers of dust.

"Cemetery Bookshop...1925." Fleur's eyebrows raised as she held the candle closer to the pictures and started to blow away the remaining dust. Every single one had Lord Raspbone besides two women, one older and one younger. Etched into each was tiny writing scrawled in black ink: Lord Raspbone, Lady Raspbone and Agatha Raspbone.

A high, pitched scream blared from within the darkness, causing the candle's flame to whip back and forth. Fleur's eyes widened. She took a step forward and held out the candle; a spider made its way down the central bookshelf, leaving a trail of web neatly decorated across the dusty tomes and started to scurry across the stone floor. It stopped just at the edge of the candle light as a delicate tapping started from within the darkness. Fleur took another step forward. The tapping stopped as Fleur stared at the floor where the spider was; busy scurrying around in a circle, it seemed to be entranced by a greyish mass. As Fleur continued to tread closer, she finally realised what the grey mass was – a human toe. It stopped tapping as the spider scurried into the darkness. There was a crunch and a giggle. Fleur gasped. An ice-cold blast tickled up the back of her neck as she heard something whisper in her ear,

"Shhh…"

Fleur spun around. Nothing. Another ice-cold blast to the back of her neck.

"No lights…"

She spun around again to see two bloodshot eyes staring at her from within the darkness; what skin was visible was tight and grey, hidden by straggly auburn hair. The figure grinned widely, its yellow teeth making Fleur gag as it brought up a finger, topped with a split, crusty nail to its lips.

Fleur was frozen solid. The figure took a step forward and Fleur shut her eyes. After a few moments, the smell of death disappeared, so she reopened them. From her right-hand side, she heard a rasping, deep voice,

"We told you. No LIGHTS!"

Another blood curdling scream as the candle blew out. Fleur sprinted into the dark, clammy hands held out to feel the way. A series of clunks echoed behind her as something stalked her every move past the bookshelves, gradually increasing speed. Fleur caught her foot and crashed into a bookshelf. Several heavy, dusty tomes cascaded down on her as she hit the stone floor with bone shattering force. As she heaved, struggling to breathe, hunched over on her knees, Fleur could see her breath freezing in front of her as the clunking came to a stop, immediately behind her. She lashed out.

"Leave me alone!"

She peered into the darkness, searching for movement. There was only silence. Her breath returned to normal, as she took a few more blasts on the inhaler. That icy feeling had gradually been replaced with an unusual warmth, which reminded Fleur of camping by the lake in Zurich as a child; the familiar scents of freshly cut grass, budding tulips and fresh water brought a smile to her face.

"Okay Fleur. Get a grip. This is all in your head. You just need to find another way out."

As her eyes adjusted, Fleur started to make out an old, boarded up window. A tiny flicker of light was struggling to find a way through the barrier. After pulling and heaving, there was a crack as the boards tore away in Fleur's hands, allowing a mercury coloured beam to illuminate most of the bookshop. Fleur's mouth was wide as she surveyed the room; despite its unmanaged state, the bookshop was a magnificent sight, its Victorian detailing along the walls and ceiling, coupled with a wrought iron winding staircase towards the end of the central bookshelf, where every step and inch had a unique carving welded on, carried such magnitude. Fleur shook her head,

"I cannot believe we're just going to knock this place down." She paused before starting to fan herself, face moist with sweat.

The clunking sound restarted. Fleur froze, her eyes stretched as far to their corners as they could manage, without turning around. She tentatively took steps towards the staircase, left leg then right leg, breathing deeply and rapidly. Every step closer she got, the warmer it became.

"Fleur, baby?"

Fleur spun around to find a silhouette, but she couldn't quite make out the features.

"Rosie? Why are you here? How did you find me?"

"Come here baby. I need to hold you."

Fleur shook her head and took a step back.

"I'm cold baby…" repeated the silhouette.

"No. You're not Rosie. Get out of my head!" Fleur yelled, taking several more steps back. She reached out and felt the handrail of the staircase. The silhouette grew completely still as Fleur was frozen to the spot. Without warning, the silhouette inclined its head to look at the source of light, before catapulting itself onto the window, morphing into an odd, black mass. Fleur was transfixed as its body rippled, swaying back and forth on the wall like a cobra would, waiting to pounce. Fleur turned and sprinted up the staircase.

Clang.

Clang.

Clang.

As she reached the top, panting and puffing, she took a further blast on the inhaler before turning and staring to the bottom of the staircase, desperately trying to control her breathing.

Clunk.

Clunk.

Clunk.

For several moments, she could only hear the frantic ticking of her heartbeat. Then a greyish, aged hand was placed delicately on the bottom step. Fleur froze, her breath completely taken away. A second hand joined it as the same bloodshot eyes peered up at her,

"Why are you running? We're all so cold."

Fleur took several, small steps backwards, hands outstretched to feel for anything that she could protect herself with, while her focus remained dead in front of her, eyes unblinking.

Bump.

She felt the wall gently align with her back. She let out a short, sharp gasp, but quickly placed her hand over her mouth.

Clunk.
>*Clunk.*
>>*Clunk.*

The sound moved up the staircase, step by agonising step, ringing out with relentless momentum. Fleur waited, hand still over her mouth as the clunking reached the top most turn of the staircase, expecting to see those eyes.

Moments passed without any flicker of movement or sound. Feeling around in the dark, Fleur's fingers wrapped around what she managed to find first, a robust book. She pressed forward, book held aloft, ready to strike. She reluctantly poked her head out over the top of the staircase. Nothing. Her hands started to burn, and she yelped, dropping the book. It had suddenly grown red hot and hissed as it hit the cold, stone floor. Fleur kicked it a few times, nudging it along the floor. Nothing. It was back to normal. She reached down and picked it up, walking over to a nearby table, where she rested it and stared at the front cover. Unlike the rest of the books in this place, it had no sign of wear or tear nor any dust along its spine or front; despite the practically zero levels of light, Fleur could still make out a rich, burgundy hue to the book, with a soft, velvet touch. There was no illustration or title to the book, on any of the sides.

"Strange."

She flipped open the cover and found a few lines of ink scribbled on the inside cover. Fleur repeated softly,

"This place is cursed. My family are cursed. Get out now while you still have time…"

Fleur moved her finger along the darker blotches that were drizzled down the rest of the page; sticky to the touch, Fleur saw a deep red tint to it.

"Oh my god!" She frantically rubbed her hand up and down her coat, the substance eventually coming off. She noticed more black fingerprints on the edges of the pages. Flipping through them, she read each one aloud, one after the other,

"Day 1: Today we moved into Raspbone Manor. It's a beautiful place. Mother and Father are happy to have the family home back. It's nice to see them smiling again. There's a bookshop on the edge of the grounds. It's where I found this diary. It belonged to my new friend. She lives in the bookshop.

Day 7: Father was not pleased that I went into the bookshop. He said it's not safe. It was built on an old cemetery. I don't

see the problem, I like talking to the dead people. They're friendly. My cough doesn't hurt me in there. I like it.

Day 30: Mother was only trying to protect me, but Father didn't like it. He's locked her in the bookshop, but I can't help her. I see her sometimes in the window looking out. Father says he will board them up if she doesn't start to behave. My cough is much worse. I'm struggling to breathe.

Day 60: It was Mother's funeral today. Father didn't cry. I didn't cry, but that's because I know Mother lives in the bookshop now with all my friends. I'm going to run away tonight to be with Mother.

Day 75: Father can't get in the bookshop. My new friend keeps him out. She's nice, even though she doesn't like the light. It hurts her. My cough has completely gone now. I finally feel happy, even though I'm still scared of Father.

Day 90: Mother hasn't spoken to me since I've been here. My friend tells me she is still hiding, waiting for me to join her, whatever that means. I am feeling weaker now and my friend seems different. She's like a black blob wherever there's some *light. It's scary. She doesn't want Father to join us. Maybe I will let Father in tomorrow. I want to leave.*

Day 91: I let Father in. She is not happy. Father brought a torch and oil. It's really hot and we can't escape. My cough is even worse. I'm going to hide this diary and come back when it's safe."

Fleur laid the book down and took a deep breath.

"What is going on here?"

It wasn't until the cold snap rang back along her spine that she started to realise that the air had grown arctic once more. Fleur started to shake. She could see a dark form in the corner of her eye.

"Please help us. We're so cold." The same rasping voice as before.

Fleur swallowed and closed her eyes.

"One. Two. Three..." She turned her head to the right; stood side by side were the two women from the picture and despite their greyish skin and straggly hair, they were holding hands. They took a step forward, their long, black gowns swaying back and forth.

"Help us. She's coming."

"Lady Raspbone and...Agatha?"

"She's coming..."

"Who's coming? Your friend?" Fleur held the diary out in front of her. Faces twisting and bodies writhing in agony, the two women started to shriek, their eyes rolling into the back of their heads. Fleur lowered the book and the shrieking started to fade.

"Destroy the book. She's coming…" The two women faded into the darkness, leaving Fleur alone again, the hairs on her arms standing to attention.

"Destroy the book? How?" Her questions yielded only silence as the surrounding black suffocated her senses.

"The light. She hates the light…" Fleur repeated.

No sooner had the words escaped her lips than the familiar rasping breath crept up on her; the stench of aged clothes whipped together with decay made her gag. Fleur felt her feet leave the ground as the black mass dragged her by the hair across the landing towards a heat that felt like hellfire itself. Floating, suspended by rippling black tentacles, Fleur looked evil in the eye, a maelstrom of darkness and decay. The mass rippled and swayed back and forth, its grip tightening around Fleur's hair. She felt weak and her eyes began to droop.

"What are you? What do you want?" Her words left her mouth like a blob of marshmallow.

The black mass started to transform the top half of its body; a young girl's face protruded out, eyes blacker than the deepest mine and she spoke with that rasping, drawn out rattle,

"Submission. We feast."

"We?" Fleur gasped, trying to claw at her captor's grip. "There are more of you?"

The mass rippled, its form pushing out spikes as the face formed a menacing smile,

"We are one. We grow strong. We feast."

Fleur threw her hands in front of her to shield herself as the mass started to wrap itself around her entire body. Screams muffled, Fleur felt lighter than air and memories of Rosie came flooding to her. There she was, stood feet away, hands outstretched as the black mass continued its freezing frenzy. Without warning, the black mass shrieked and Rosie disappeared. Fleur crashed to the floor dazed, as she saw a long, flowing dressing gown stood above her holding the diary aloft, a brilliant white light blasted from within its pages.

"Back evil, to the black pit you originated from." The black mass writhed and lashed out, morphing from one shape to another; Rosie, Agatha, Lady Raspbone and even Lord Raspbone appeared. It started to shrink and retreat to the shadows.

"No evil, you will not escape."

Lord Raspbone's attention turned to something in the darkness. A smile appeared.

"Agatha, Margaret, I'm sorry for my mistakes. I have lived with this pain for long enough."

Fleur blinked and rubbed the side of her head, staring at Lord Raspbone.

"What?" She uttered, groggily.

Agatha and Lady Raspbone, both had returned to their original appearance, stepped out of the darkness, hand in hand, a beautiful white aura surrounding them. They turned their attention to the black mass as they stood side by side with Lord Raspbone and directed their light at the beast, which writhed and screamed before taking large chunks out of the bookshop's ceiling and floor as it lashed out. It started to bury deep down, throwing stone and wood around before the upper landing started to buckle, throwing Fleur over the side. The last thing she remembered was the beast descending into the floor, fire gushing out as its screams disappeared deep underground, before everything went black.

*   *   *   *

The light rain trickled down the window as the sun's morning beams gently woke Fleur from her slumber; emerald eyes shining, she stretched and wiped the sleep away, slowly regaining her focus as the Raspbone Manor kitchen became clearer. Sat on the chair across from her was Lord Raspbone, taking dainty sips from his cup. His eyebrows raised when he noticed Fleur moving,

"Ah good, you're awake."

"What happened?"

"Now that is a question. Come with me and I'll finish the story for you…"

"No way," Fleur interjected, shaking her head. She attempted to stand, stumbling slightly.

"Careful." Lord Raspbone held out a hand to steady Fleur, who shook him off. "You have nothing to worry about from me. I must apologise for my earlier misdemeanour. My daughter and wife have now moved on and are at peace, thanks to you Miss Davids. For that, I am forever grateful."

"You're grateful? You locked me in an old, stinking bookshop with…with…" She struggled, mouth wide open.

"I don't even know what to call that thing…I just need to leave. I need my phone. Give me my things." Fleur held out her hand, continuing to thrust it at Lord Raspbone, who bit his bottom lip and furrowed his brow.

"About that…"

Fleur waved her hand dismissively and strode towards the backdoor, grabbing the handle. She shook it several times, rattling it with such force, the handle broke off. Fleur stepped back, handle in hand and inclined her head to Lord Raspbone,

"I'm sorry…" She placed it on the side and folded her arms, refusing to make eye contact. There was a tentative pause.

"There are things you need to see Miss Davids."

Lord Raspbone's tone caused Fleur to turn her head. Her face went deathly pale and she fell over her feet at the horror that sat at the table; a corpse coloured a terrible dirt brown was sat at Lord Raspbone's chair, mouth open as if in a state of perpetual agony wearing Lord Raspbone's dressing grown, which was moth eaten and grubby. Lord Raspbone continued to stand next to the corpse, staring at Fleur with a stony face, as he stirred his cup with a tiny, silver spoon.

"What is that?" Fleur gestured to the corpse, pushing herself back as far as possible to the wall. Lord Raspbone pointed at his own chest.

"But...but, I spoke to you on the phone. How? No, this is a dream. Wake up Fleur, Wake up!"

"For one hundred years I have been feeding that thing in the bookshop, waiting for a chance to banish it and free my wife and daughter, but the chances were few and far between." His eyes flicked to look at Fleur, "Until you, Fleur..."

"But YOU did that to your daughter and your wife. You did this."

Lord Raspbone chuckled and took another sip from his cup, raising his right eyebrow,

"Is that what the diary told you?"

Fleur nodded. Lord Raspbone placed his cup and saucer on the table and walked out of the room, only to return moments later carrying the large diary. Its velvety surface was burned and gnarled. He dropped it on the table with a thud.

"It lies and likes to trick people. Well, it used to before you came along. For some reason, it trusted you. It hasn't been so open to an individual since…"

He paused.

"Agatha?" Fleur offered. Lord Raspbone nodded, hand to his mouth.

"I tried to save them both, but the beast was too strong. I even attempted to reduce the bookshop to ashes, but the beast merely allowed the flames to consume my beautiful girls, protecting the bookshop and continuing its insatiable appetite. It was like a buffet for it, attracted by all the dead buried in the cemetery below."

Fleur's face softened, her arms relaxing, fists unclenched.

"So how come you weren't trapped in there too – when did you...?"

"Die? I managed to escape, barely, but the beast had inflicted enough damage for me to die here. Trapped forever."

"Why haven't you moved on?"

Lord Raspbone pointed at his corpse, specifically to a large burn mark across the torso.

"The beast marked me. It grabbed me and started to consume my life force. It's what stops you from moving on to wherever you go…" He looked down at his feet in silence, before refocusing on Fleur,

"But I'm used to it now…so…"

"Wait!" Fleur stepped forward. "The beast did the same thing to me, but I'm here, I'm fine."

Lord Raspbone's eyes flickered and he averted her gaze. Fleur tilted her head, waiting. Her host sighed and beckoned her to follow. They made their way into a side room; the silk curtains were partly drawn, allowing a sliver of light into the dimly lit space. Sat up in the corner, was Fleur's body, pale and still, a black burn slashed across her chest.

"No, no, no. This can't be happening. No, no, no…"

"I'm sorry, my dear. But I believe the diary would only show itself to those...already dead."

Fleur stumbled backwards, knocking a small cabinet over. Ignoring the crashing, Fleur turned and ran. She ran from room to room, trying every door, but all were locked. Eventually she made her way to the entrance hall and threw open the double doors and ran into the courtyard. She took no notice of the state of the bookshop, which had been completely ravaged by the beast during its descent, only a slight wisp of smoke could be seen where the old building had once stood. Fleur could see the winding road that led down to the gated entrance and sprinted with all her remaining energy.

"This is a dream. This is not real. I need to get back to Rosie."

As she reached the wrought iron gates, she grabbed hold of the handle. She stopped and put her hand on her chest. Her breathing was normal.

"No, wait. This isn't right. Oh no, please no..."

She pulled the gate with all her strength and stepped over the threshold. Blinding white light enveloped her and she shielded her eyes. She stopped running and removed her hands from her face.

"No..."

Fleur was stood in the kitchen of Raspbone Manor, Lord Raspbone stirring his cup and shaking his head, a sorrowful look on his face.

"I'm sorry my dear, but there is no escape. You died the night the bridge collapsed. I found you and brought you here. I needed your help."

"Rosie!" Fleur screamed as she pressed her face to the window.

*   *   *   *

Rosie Tanner stood over the collapsed bridge, huddled up in a bright, green overcoat, her mousey, curly hair flapping in the strong wind. Her face was solemn, but her eyes still twinkled as if they were powered by everlasting hope. She held her phone in her hands, checking the last message she received from Fleur Davids a few hours before. Rosie turned as footsteps approached from behind.

"I'm sorry Miss Tanner, but we only found the car. No body. We will continue the search." Officer Thomas said, attempting to improve the situation with a smile. Rosie shook her head, a solitary tear meandering down her ivory cheek.

"She's dead. I can feel it."

THE END

L - #0070 - 191218 - C0 - 210/148/6 - PB - DID2397015